NEW SEED AND HARD GROUND

THE SUMMONING OF HEARTS

A Novella
Book 1 of The New Seed Series

CHARLES ANTHONY SOLORIO

Printed in the United States of America

Print ISBN: 9781951490829
E-Book ISBN: 9781951490836

Canoe Tree
Press

4697 Main Street
Manchester Center, VT 05255

Canoe Tree Press is a division of DartFrog Books.

Acknowledgments

I would like to thank the Author who inspired this story and all great stories.

Thank you Claire for the love, support, and sacrifices. There was much and many.

To Rebekah for the opinions and ideas that challenged mine.

To Caleb for the many conversations that influenced me and the story.

Thank you to family, Patrick, Dori, Kathy, and all the readers, friends, and co-workers who helped shape me and my journey in this bigger story we all dwell in.

PROLOGUE

Greetings to my brothers and sisters in hiding,

The Story read me and called me into new pages hidden and forbidden by those who hunt us.

A single word called me inside, and I stepped into a new scene. For the first time, I had no fear of being killed by our country's leaders. Censored scenes from ancient past, present, and future moved in my mind, unveiled before my eyes.

I am now fully awake.

I now know the secret they hid from us.

I am guilty of treason.

The calling voice of the Story's Author, a mere whisper above the daily screams, will be forever impaled into my memory, like a deep sword that pierced the hard ground.

I will never forget the Voice.

I thought we would never forget the Holocaust.

And now, behind the walls of labor camp CA 57JC, in the midst of the continuing ancient hunt, I await my murder.

How did we not hear the voices of the hunted from days of ancient past? How did we not see the connection between all the millions killed, hidden in plain sight, through the ages to today?

But... someone awakened me. Someone from before the beginning of history placed something into me for today. And it cannot be annihilated. I am commissioned to reveal this Story to you.

You should know, my brothers and sisters, that though I live in the twenty-first century, the origin of my Story goes back to before the beginning. The Author smuggled illegal contraband and wove it into my DNA before I was born. I did not know it would one day cause me both new life and my murder.

For my first few decades, I just wanted to live my own life. I lived ignorant of what was within me. The contraband lay dormant within.

Protected.

Living.

Waiting.

Since I was a young boy, a gnawing sense that something was very wrong in our world grew within me. Even when I closed my eyes to escape, I could still see it. When I hid in seclusion, it was still there.

My eyes opened partway.

Then the dream was put into my head. A recurring nightmare haunted me almost every night. I heard voices crying out. I sought solace and solution and met others in the underground who experienced similar things.

My eyes opened further.

When I was asleep in my first life, I lived as a useful idiot for the oppressive kings. I thought if they were not aware of me and only harassed others, then

I was in peace. In the perpetual pain of this world, I lived as an adult toddler seeking that which temporarily distracted me or abated my base desires.

I resisted those who dwelled in the mobile underground when they tried to teach me from the Author's book of treason. Why would I risk my life with a banned book that has killed millions over centuries?

During my last secret meeting with the illegal mobile underground, I grabbed one of their illegal books to report the subversives to the authorities. I ran to avoid the look of my betrayal upon their faces. I did not want to hear their cries for mercy before their executions. I ran until I could no longer run.

But something stopped me. A single word echoed in my head. The dropped book lay open, staring at me. I then had what I can only describe as an encounter. I still do not possess the words to describe what I saw. All I know is it offended me in my walking sleep state minutes away from reporting the mobile underground to the authorities. I saw something that shook my inner core of being. I questioned everything I thought I knew in my old life. My hard heart ground cracked wide open.

A seed was placed into the gaping hole.

My feet stopped moving, and I could not run. My eyes went dark. My hands clawed at the air, searching for something to hold on to. I could no longer trust the eyes I had always trusted. Were my feet still on the ground? My world flipped upside down, and I fell onto a large rock in front of a garden store.

My eyes were open, but I could not see.

Then in my mind, flashing images. Glimpses of history censored from our textbooks passed before my dark eyes. I saw an Adversary moving through his henchmen in the shadows and in the wide open.

I can tell you now that the Adversary roams our land, devouring all, through all, in all generations. Every one of his strategies and effects hidden before us in plain sight.

I lay sprawled on the ground. My sight returned. Blood stained my shirt, though I had no cut.

The henchmen—power-hungry hunting murderers—appeared in my mind again out from the shadows and into a different light. A very different light. I felt compassion for the ones hunting us. A love for our murderers! How can this be?

The Author of the book of treason asks me to love those who murder us?

Months after the encounter, they captured my family and me. They did unspeakable things to us. It was as if they removed parts of our bodies, seeking to cut out the Author's Story knitted within us. I pleaded with them to stop. I proclaimed to their faces that even with our deaths, what was of the Author's could never be destroyed.

But they could not listen. I asked them to kill me and spare my wife and children. They laughed and spat on me and ripped my wife out of my arms. Never have I been so weak. The rest of us huddled together and locked arms as we screamed for them to stop.

They slowly executed my wife before my eyes. Before my children's eyes. They then ripped one child at a time from our locked arms. They killed my children.

They laughed at me as they spilled their blood. I heaved, trying to breathe. I reached out to my wife and children, no longer moving. They laughed at me when I broke from them and collapsed onto my family's spilled blood.

My spilled blood.

They tortured me with a million deaths, as they left me to live—to die. I rot daily with my memories and regrets, alone behind these prison walls. I cannot rip out of my ears the sounds of others from surrounding rooms.

This is not a labor camp.

It is a single concentration camp, amongst many others.

They feed me just enough to not fully die, to prolong my time remembering my family's last cries and to hear the perpetual daily ones around me.

And I am supposed to love and see all my enemies in a new light?

They told me tomorrow they will spare me the future pain of what my eyes will yet see by ripping out my eyes. Today is the last day I will see with my eyes. If my letter and the writings have found you, I pray that your eyes can see what I am to reveal to you.

Brothers and sisters, be warned of the cost. Many want to kill you before you awaken and open your eyes or before you attempt to awaken others. If you desire to be awake, then know all that you have previously known will be greatly disturbed. Your life will be turned upside down, and you will fall on a great stone. If you ask for the seed to open your eyes to the Story hidden within you and choose to believe the Author's Story, you will be hunted.

Are you willing to give away your life? Do you want to know the Story under the ever-present shadow of death that hunts us?

I pray that you desire to be awake, for the Author does not abandon His Story or those of His within it.

We give thanks to the Author and His book of treason. We have gathered all the sacred writings. He assisted us greatly and provided some of the secret parts of the Story unknown to most. We give our thanks to all those revealed in the following pages.

Thank you, Joseph and Emma and the house churches worldwide in hiding. Where would we be without the Assembled? Ellie told us of amazing things as the Author indwelled in her and enabled her. Blessings and many thanks to you, Ellie.

All hidden and seen parts of the Story are submitted under the authority of the Author speaking to us in the living book of treason. I am thankful, and mournful, of all the millions who have died for this revelation, now passed on to you.

I am but a common man. You are precious in what sight I have left. My beloved, you do not yet fully know that you dwell in the midst of the Story. In the difficult days ahead, remember the Story hidden and now surfaced in me is in you. Perhaps you do not have a recurring nightmare or hear the voices crying out in it, but in times of quiet, someone calls out to you to step inside.

You know all this to be true.

Even without my eyes, I will see love win. Ask for the seed to plant itself within you to open your eyes to see the Author's Story hidden within.

I now give you all the writings, with considerable help from one of our spies. I share with you but a splinter of the hope found in the epic framework of the Story we dwell in.

The Adversary roams our land seeking to deceive and devour. The cries of those hunted by the Adversary still echo today. Thorns continue to proliferate, and our heart ground hardens more. It cracks in our darkness, daily drought, and famine. With the garden left unattended, what else can grow but the weeds and thorns of self, vengeance, rage, hate, and unforgiveness?

But this is not the end. There is a hope and a love soon to be revealed to you. What a grand adventure awaits you in the coming pages!

Are these the last words my eyes will ever see?

If you continue to read, if you believe, you will see part of a grand mystery of love revealed and the secret hope unveiled.

By the grace of the Author, you will see what was placed in you. Light will penetrate through the deep cracks of wounds in your drought and famine-stricken heart ground.

There it is.

Underneath the thick layer of thorns covering the hard ground.

I can see it in you.

Down below.

Deep.

Hidden and protected.

A seedling...

I love you, my brothers and sisters.

Pablo

Chapter 1

In the beginning, within the midst of vast moving galaxies and swirling stars, a great light revealed a single speck. Upon this outpost, a Father spoke into existence a small remote settlement for His two offspring in a beautiful garden.

It was very good. The Father loved His children. The children loved their Father.

But their Father had an Enemy.

The Adversary.

The Adversary plotted the coming hunt in the garden.

Seduced and deceived by the Enemy of their Father, the children rejected their Father. The Adversary infiltrated and colonized the children's hearts to then colonize others to live under his rule.

The Adversary moved through the Father's children and polluted and contaminated the garden paradise. Death intruded upon life for the first time.

But the Father was not idle in the garden. A new seed had already been planted.

He cast out His broken children from the garden. Over the years, the still-present Father sent His children out into new settlements to reveal the voice of the Father, calling all His children to return to Him.

But the children resisted the call and often sent

out their own settlements to all the lands of the world to feed their own desires. Over the years, the voices of the many afflicted by the Adversary and his followers cried out.

Near the end of the sixteenth century, a nation sent one hundred colonists and four hundred soldiers to Africa to start the colony of Luanda.

Men and women sought a new land.

Adventure.

Families wanted a new start.

Some were soldiers ordered to take away the land from the natives.

Some were seeking silver and gold.

The gathering cries of the afflicted from days past still echo today. They warn us of both an approaching horrific evil and a Hope that cannot ever be hunted down.

CHAPTER 2

CHINASA

Africa 1605

She pulled the hand off her mouth as the voices screaming in the nightmare awoke her again.

She opened her eyes in the middle of another night, not knowing where she was.

Once again, since her childhood, there was no hand covering her mouth.

It was disturbing enough to wake up every night thinking she was drowning in the ocean. But hearing her son Pada's single crying voice disappear over the ocean horizon was what made Chinasa tremble.

The hairs on the back of her neck stood up. The imagined hand over her mouth reminded her that something was coming their way. Something was on the hunt.

She gasped for air, as if surfacing from underwater for a long-awaited breath.

Am I going crazy? Where are my boys? Where are Pada and Okoro?

She resumed breathing with the comforting snoring next to her.

But the voices, the cries for help, echoed in her head in a chaotic harmony. They came from different directions in all languages. They seemed to rise from thousands of points on the ground, from the air, even from underground.

Whom could she talk to about hearing her son's voice above the thousands of others crying out in a recurring nightmare? Whom could she talk to about her ongoing search for a sense of home and about the foreboding of evil roaming the land coming their way? Her husband, Okoro, already thought she was mad with all her praying and talking about God.

She could not stay awake every night to prevent the nightmare from entering her head again. Even the fear of falling asleep could not keep her awake all night.

Though they were only in their twenties, Chinasa and Okoro always said they would one day grow old with their grandchildren in the outskirts of Luanda. They would one day die here. But this nightmare was changing everything about what she thought was her family's future. Why wasn't Okoro having the same dream so they could agree on at least one thing in life?

Where could they go? Luanda was supposed to be the only home they ever knew. What kind of life would she have if she could not control where she wanted to live? Somebody had to hold on to a stable home for their children's sake. This had to be home.

But would they have to leave? No more gazing upon the beautiful ocean birds flying above to wherever they desired. No more gazing on the beautiful beaches with the perfect water in those hot months. No more relief from the scorching sun that was more punishing inland than on the coast. Where would they go? She had no other family. Okoro was just now finding the consistent work that he had promised years ago when they'd courted. He would not want to move now.

And what about little Pada? Even before Chinasa had married, she'd known her future son's destiny was to start here at home, near Luanda. This was where the New World would start, and Pada was going to play a role in the new future, the new hope, for their people.

But she could not escape the gnawing in the back of her mind that prevented restful sleep and spilled over into her days. If they remained, they would be unable to outrun what was soon coming after them. Like a hunter finding a wounded animal that waited too long to start running, they would be cornered and trapped.

If they did not escape when they had time, little Pada would not grow up to change the world. She would be a failure as a mother. She would miss out on what she was created to do. If she remained silent and did not tell Okoro why they needed to move, the blood of her family would forever stain her hands. What good would it be for Okoro to have a job when they no longer had their lives?

Breathe. Breathe. Breathe.

Fully awake, her eyes adjusted to the darkness in their hut. All was as it should be in the stillness of a warm and sticky moonlit night. Okoro still snored like he always did. Her little boy, Pada, lay dead asleep. She took her three deep breaths and said her three prayers just to make sure.

Fading sleep brought fading good health. Yesterday, she'd staggered and momentarily fallen asleep while walking Pada home. Her chest sometimes ached. Her thinking reminded her of the thick fog that sometimes rolled inland. Occasionally her legs buckled while she carried Pada when he needed comfort. Protecting her boy every moment of every day meant no rest when she was awake. Friends moved away because of rumors of what was coming to their village on the outskirts of Luanda. All of which could keep anyone awake at night—even without the voices.

She sighed. Time was up and no time to rest, with her family vulnerable and evil on its way.

Being tall in a small hut with two others inside, she hesitated to rise and disturb her boys. Being thin these days though, from a lack of appetite, made it easier to maneuver within the tight spaces.

There was no more time for prayer here. She staggered to her feet—flattened more than ever before, as if carrying something heavy since Pada was born. Even with numb and calloused feet, the hardness of the ground vibrated up her body. There was no going back to sleep this night.

Thankfulness filled her heart that it was safe to walk to her tree in the canyon outside her village. She stepped into the middle of the night. She passed the neighbor's garden that hadn't produced anything fruitful in months. Refuge and scary mystery dwelled in the canyon ahead of her. Though remote enough for privacy, shadows seemed to hide and wait when the sun or moon sat just right in the sky. The shadows infiltrated even more with the moon out. She often prayed for Okoro and Pada in the middle of her sleepless nights. But hearing her little boy's voice disappear over the horizon in a nightmare was reason enough never to allow Pada to wander away alone to the canyon. If she struggled with knowing where her sense of home was, she would not let Pada walk away from what he knew as his only home.

Something is coming. I can feel it. How can I protect him? It will not always be possible for me to be with him. I know I heard my boy's voice disappear onto the sea.

Out of nervous habit, she squinted her eyes and then opened them fully as a beautiful breeze caressed her cheeks. The gentle breeze rustled the thatched roofs of the huts to the broken rhythm of her footsteps, joining her in the night.

There it was. Under the light of the moon, the worn-out path to her tree. She walked to the large baobab tree and placed a small piece of wood she carried at its base, along with her three prayers.

In a quiet moment before her tree, a thought seemed to be planted into her mind. Like words bridging one conversation into a future one. Verses from the New Testament that a friend had quoted under this same tree weeks before. She had ignored the verses at the time, as they had no relevance to her prayers then.

The verses returned.

Why these words?

They returned a third time.

She pulled out a graphite stick and paper one of the Portuguese ladies had given her, from England. She wrote the words down on the folded piece of paper she always carried with her and then read them.

Then Herod secretly called the Magi and determined from them the exact time the star appeared. And he sent them to Bethlehem and said, "Go and search carefully for the Child; and when you have found him, report to me, so that I too may come and worship him."

She lifted her head to the dark moonlit sky and opened her hands, holding the words and another small piece of wood.

Herod hunting down the child Jesus? My Lord, what are you saying? Why these words? Why for this time?

I summon hearts every day.

What was that?

In the silent night, the mild breeze strengthened into a gentle wind. Dust arose and swirled like a figure forming next to her. Then all was still.

She'd always thought that God communicated with her through dreams, visions, and general impressions. But never as a voice in her head. It was different from all the other voices. Gentle. But with more force. It had a weight to it. It brought peace.

After a lengthy conversational prayer, she walked home with new energy. Yes, evil approached, but thanks to her diligence, her family was untouched. She could live with the exchange of lost sleep for the answered memorized prayers of safety for her family.

Even with the renewed hope of someone hearing her prayers, she still had her questions. What was she to do with the nightmare and voices? Where was she to go? Whom could she talk to?

After more prayer back at her hut, while Okoro and Pada slept, it was time to start the morning. She woke her boys up and asked Okoro to take Pada to run and play nearby, as she would need to summon any remaining strength to go to the village market.

She tried to nap as her boys ate breakfast and dressed for the day. She lay down exhausted but unable to sleep. Just before Okoro and Pada left, she said, "Please watch Pada carefully. I would never forgive myself if something ever happened when I should have been there protecting him."

Okoro rolled his eyes and stepped outside of their hut with Pada.

She moaned and pushed her hands off her thighs to stand up. Okoro was a good protector, and now peace and quiet joined her in the hut. Though she still wrestled with guilt over not watching Pada, she enjoyed her trips to the market as a respite from caring for an energetic boy. She relished her alone times in the canyon, but being amongst those in her community always revived her, and the village market contained a great sampling of her people. Truth be told, she loved to hear the latest gossip of her neighbors and those she did not know.

She started her second walk of the young day before some in her village had even stepped outside. A short distance away from where they gathered to buy and trade for food, something caught her eye. Even though it was still early, this morning was different. It was worse than the previous week.

Where is everyone?

It was more obvious this morning. There were fewer people out shopping than usual. Could fewer people need to eat? It really was true. People were moving away from the village one by one. Off to her side, her friend Nkiru walked to the market. Chinasa moved toward her friend, when a man bumped into her. *Is he blind, or did he run into me on purpose?*

"I am sorry. I did not see you," Chinasa said as the man stopped in front of her. He blocked her from moving forward. He stood facing her with wide-open unblinking eyes and did not reply.

Something was wrong with him.

Chinasa turned her head back and forth. A rare silence enclosed her and the man as the others in the area focused on bartering and purchasing food and leaving as soon as possible. If the man pulled out a knife, she was on her own. No one could help her in time. She stepped back to give herself a little more time if he made a dangerous move. Her hands throbbed in rhythm with her chest rising and falling, waiting for any sudden movement. They remained facing each other in silence. She had never seen him before, yet his eyes were both empty of life and vaguely familiar. And he also seemed filled with something foreign to her human experience.

"Do I know you?" she asked.

He smiled and made strange grunting noises. She would have felt safer with a thief trying to take something from her, for at least she would know the man's intent. But this person stood with a foreign purpose, which made him unpredictable. Perhaps even capable of killing or maiming? Or *was* he a thief?

Was he trying to take *her* away?

His smile disappeared. His eyes widened, as if he saw a monster right behind her.

What was he scared of?

Should *she* be scared of what was standing behind her? She slowly turned her head away from him to glance over her shoulder while still trying to watch the crazy man from the corner of her eye. She expected to find what frightened the man but did not see anyone immediately behind her. She lost focus of him, and as she turned her head back, he grabbed her arm and pulled.

The grip of pain ached down her arm. She stood frozen with her eyes locked on his hand, which pulsated as he squeezed harder. She remembered the hand she imagined over her mouth again that morning. Her arm throbbed in an apprehended rhythm with another beat. She tried to move her arm but could not break free. After a long pause, she shifted her eyes away from his pulsating hand and back toward him. His body twitched as his lips quivered in a broken smile. His eyes had darkened more after grabbing her arm. Something familiar stared back at her behind the absence of light in his eyes.

"Let go," she demanded as the man grunted. He did not let go but squeezed harder. Chinasa opened her mouth but could not force the back of her throat into a scream.

Her friend Nkiru walked up to the man as his eyes widened. He trembled, as if what he was afraid of was now inside Nkiru. She yanked his hand off of Chinasa.

In her mind, she saw a flash of someone grabbing her arm when she was young, and then the scene disappeared. Chinasa resumed breathing.

What was that?

Others gathered around them to make sure the man stopped his attack. Someone shoved the twitching man away from Chinasa. His eyes narrowed, and he made a strange unhuman sound and stepped away while locking his gaze on Chinasa.

Nkiru hugged Chinasa and whispered in her ear, "Are you all right?"

"I saw something in him... I saw something I have never seen, yet... it was familiar," Chinasa whispered as she stared off into the distance.

"You are okay now. We will not let him hurt you."

"Should we report him?" Chinasa asked as she rubbed her arm.

"He is no threat. He is just crazy," an onlooker said.

"People like him have always been around—though this one is new," another said. "When enough people complain, they might take him away, and he would just come back here anyway."

Chinasa and her friend walked away together. "Do you know him?" Nkiru asked.

"I have never seen him before. Did you see his eyes?" Chinasa asked as she shook her head.

Nkiru kept her focus on the strange man. "He looked like he was trying to stop you from doing something... or trying to take you away."

"They are right. He is just crazy. Okoro would think I was crazy if I thought this was anything more than a crazy man acting crazy." Chinasa brushed herself off and tried to ignore the man. He made a quick movement, as if to grab her again, and Chinasa jumped. The man laughed and stared at her.

Why is he looking at my stomach?

There was a lengthy quiet pause, though Chinasa's heart still raced. "How are you and your family these days?" Chinasa asked as her friend jumped.

Nkiru put her hand on her chest and gave a small laugh. "I am sorry. You startled me." She paused. "That man is still looking at you. As if you are some sort of a threat to him. This morning my thoughts are elsewhere." Nkiru shook her head and looked all around. "It is as if my head is already somewhere else and my body is all that remains standing. Like the chickens that pause before they run for a short while after their heads are cut off."

"I feel that way every day. But for me, it is more like a goat after it has eaten too much clothing and cannot run away from the pain in its stomach." Chinasa laughed.

The man stood at a distance. Still staring.

Nkiru's smile disappeared. "This is the last time I will see you. We are leaving this village after I pick up some food for us... Do you feel it? Can you feel what is coming?"

"Feel what?" Chinasa tilted her head and studied her friend's eyes.

"Like what has taken over that man. Something is coming and taking over. Different from what we have ever seen before. I can feel it. It is spreading on our land, and it is spreading beyond as well. I know this sounds crazy. It is like something invisible that moves through the visible."

Breathe. Breathe. Breathe. Do not scream. DO NOT SCREAM.

Chinasa took another deep breath. Someone else felt it too? "Are you saying it is like an evil spirit?" Chinasa closed her eyes. She did not want to see her friend's response.

After a lengthy pause, Chinasa dared to look.

Her friend pointed to her own chest. "Much is out of our control, but I think we bear some responsibility for what is coming. Whatever it is that is coming.

Our leaders are the consequence of growing up in a culture that thinks it can determine right and wrong based on what is convenient. They grow up to then rule the same way as they were raised. We allowed our leaders to mistreat people we don't like. That evil grew, like in every other land. We are no different. Evil has always been around—but it is growing here in a new way. This is a different evil."

Her friend paused to catch her breath and pointed to the surrounding village. "We have to go. Yet... I have so much family history—my grandparents and parents were born and died here. I was born here. I was married here. I screamed as I delivered our children here. But our family needs to leave."

How can we leave here? Pada is to change the world, starting here. But something is coming after us.

The friends paused to look around. Most people that morning were quiet and avoided the possibility of conversing with others. Talking occurred in hushed tones as villagers arrived at the market. Like there was a secret. Or something that everyone knew but did not want to talk about.

Where were most of the figs? Honey? The wheat breads? Where were the yams and eggs that could be mixed together to make delicious eto? There were even fewer coffee beans. There was less food, even with fewer people purchasing food. Even the farmers were leaving.

It was time to find out what was going on. Chinasa shifted her purpose from getting food for her family to snacking on the latest village secrets. Could she charm information out of people, fewer in number and hesitant to talk?

The strange man at a distance still stared. Sometimes he stood still. Did his eyes even blink? He occasionally made jerky movements, like something was trying to get out of him.

Nkiru wiped tears from her eyes. She said good-bye, gave one last hug, and let go of her friend.

Chinasa stood alone with one less friend. Three people nearby smelled and squeezed fruits as they talked about the changes in their village. She walked toward them, held some coffee beans, of which no one in her family liked, and eavesdropped on a nearby conversation.

A petite young woman talked with a friend about visiting the village. Chinasa looked away when the young woman turned her head, as if preparing to share a secret with her friend. The young woman paused and then leaned closer to her friend's right ear. "I have had a repeating nightmare for months. I have never had a dream like that before. I think the dream is telling us why people are leaving."

The young woman's eyes were downcast, and Chinasa turned her head back toward her.

The woman's friend shrugged her shoulders. "Everybody has dreams. What makes your dream different?"

The petite woman shook her head. "This one was real. Even during the dream, I told myself that it was not a dream. I was in a different place, living like I am now. Like I was placed somewhere else, and God put things into my head in a different language that I am not familiar with. It made me want to learn the language of the dream so I could converse with the one who put it in my head."

The young woman's friend stopped looking at people walking by and fixed her eyes on her companion. "Okay, what happened in the dream?"

The young woman put some beans down and paused. She put her face in her hands. "I just can't repeat it right now. It is too real... it is too much... many people died."

"People died? Why should imaginary people dying in a random dream matter to you?"

"Why would I be shown this?"

Chinasa wiped her forehead and then her hands. With a shaking hand, she grabbed the small piece of wood she carried with her.

I just want to go home. Don't make me talk to her. Eventually the voices will go away, and I can just rest.

No one would notice if she moved down the clear path home. No one would stop her. She would tell anyone who did stop her that she'd decided to get food next week. The boys would be okay for a few days. Her legs moved like tree trunks stuck in the ground. She paused and could only watch people mingle around her.

Please, legs. Move. Toward them or away from them. Make up your mind.

She could go home and finally rest. They had enough food already, and Okoro was getting chubby. If she took one step closer to the two women, things would never be the same.

This has to be for my family.

"I am sorry to interrupt, but can I talk with you?" Chinasa asked as she locked eyes with the woman talking about her dream.

The petite woman raised her eyebrow and looked at her friend. Silence. She then said, "I will see you later."

The companion walked away.

Chinasa rubbed her eyes with her forearm and tried to stay focused. "My name is Chinasa. What is your name?"

"My name is Abeni."

Should I share what I know? I am not sure I want to know what she knows.

They walked apart from the small crowd. Chinasa's hands trembled behind her back. "I am honored to meet you, Abeni. I know this is a strange question. Do you know that man staring at us?"

They stopped walking, and Abeni turned her head. She cleared her throat. "No. I thought he was following me earlier, but then he disappeared. Why is he bent forward and moving like that? Is there something wrong with him?"

Chinasa hid her hands behind herself again. "I don't know. He is still staring at us. But I refuse to let him distract me from telling you that..."

She leaned toward Abeni and pulled her farther from the crowd. "I have something to tell you. Something I believe will change our lives and the lives of our families."

They stood still and stared into each other's eyes. Chinasa turned her head eastward.

Abeni covered her mouth as her eyes widened. "God woke me up this morning. I knew someone was going to talk to me about—"

"We have had the same recurring dream."

All the noises of the village seemed to stop. Abeni closed her eyes. The man groaned. Chinasa tilted her head closer to Abeni. "That man does not want us to be together. He knows something that even we do not know about ourselves yet."

Abeni removed her hand from her mouth and nodded. "Our time may be short."

The man straightened up, as if an invisible chain pulled upward on his neck. He fisted his hands as he stomped toward them.

Chapter 3

ELEANOR

England 1605

It was a beautiful and wet early winter morning in Southampton. The familiar melody of the rain pounded outside, and the water dripped onto Eleanor's floor next to her bed and played its familiar song. Music and song to celebrate the promise of another day.

But Eleanor could not forget the voices in the nightmare that invaded her almost nightly. And she could not go back in time. She could not change the evil that surfaced years ago.

And today was the anniversary of what happened all those years ago.

The dark presence that visited her then was a mere foreshadowing of what now moved in a new way. She could feel it. Something was roaming the land and coming her way. How could she run away from it if it was another day in which Eleanor had difficulty moving?

I can't run away from the king and his men if my legs refuse to move.

She used reserved energy to flick her long, matted brown hair from her eyes. She bent down to move the bucket from under her bed to catch the dripping water next to her. With the slow drip, she did not have to move again for several hours if it continued raining.

She needed to get food for the week. The rain pounded down and chased all the good people off her street, but her feet could barely move in bed. She did not want to move. She needed to rest again.

Some days she gave up trying to move, and other days she willed herself to perform the most basic tasks. Some days gratefulness filled her because of the help of others, and other days she thought she wasted their time.

She found a way to sit up. A small mirror lay next to her bed, and she momentarily glimpsed at her forties. She stared at the smile lines formed so early from her youth. The same lines that did not often move now. She lay back down. Nineteen years ago—how could she not remember what had happened that night?

She tugged the worn blanket tighter. It wrapped around her like a faithful hug when in need. Her mind slipped out of the paralysis of the present and into the pain of the past. She could not stop the descent.

It was nineteen years ago to the day.

It was a typical evening back then... until the voices.

She'd awakened with the voices in her nightmare again that night. But that night she'd heard another voice above the other cries. She'd steadied her legs as she trembled and stumbled to her second-story bedroom window.

Alice?

All seemed normal at Alice's house across the street. In the ocean of surrounding voices in Eleanor's nightmare, it was Alice's singular voice above the others that awoke her. The scream resounded into the night.

But did Alice actually scream and awaken Eleanor? Or did Eleanor dream she heard her voice above the other voices? Should she run to Peter's house down the street? He would do anything for Eleanor, as he counseled her about the nightmare. He would understand.

But like someone living in a town full of thieves, Alice always seemed to hide or protect something.

Am I going crazy? Did someone scream outside? Is Alice okay?

Up and down the street, a calm exterior betrayed the existence of a storm inside Eleanor. With rain outside, a fog inside her mind clouded what she should do. She shifted her feet back and forth, toward and away from the stairs leading to her front door.

Rain with a gentle breeze floated droplets through the air. Then something moved. Alice's door opened.

A gasp in her dark bedroom made Eleanor jump, until she realized the gasp was her own.

That is strange. Alice rarely leaves her home, and not late at night.

A man stepped outside and closed the door. He swiveled his head up and down the street. Tall and thin, he hunched over, as if carrying something heavy. Did she hear him grunt as he peered at his buttons out of alignment? He adjusted his clothing with jerk-like movements and walked down the street, still turning his head back and forth. Several steps later, he was lost in the night.

Should I go and check on Alice? Is she okay? But people can disappear into the night. How can my future son arrive in this world if I disappear into the night like the many others? I don't want her to think I am a nosy neighbor watching every personal and private movement.

She returned to her bed, lay down, and closed her fluttering eyes.

But I heard her voice.

The same dream that awoke her that night to look across the street, awoke her again early that following morning.

In the dream, many people were dying of thirst in a famine and drought-stricken land. People were drowning in the ocean. Pieces of broken ships floated and sank into the sea. Cries moved out and circled over the debris and dying.

She lay in a pool of sweat on that cold morning.

I heard Alice in the ocean of voices.

She sprang out of bed and went to her window again. Alice's door was still closed from the night before. What had happened the previous night?

Eleanor dressed, wrapped herself in a blanket,

and wandered across the street. She stopped and looked back and forth between Alice's house and Peter's a few houses down.

Her faithful fiancé, Peter, was always there for her. She already considered him her fiancé. He just did not know it yet. Soon he would know. Soon he would ask her to be his bride, and soon they would be married. They would move far away from the king and his political enemies who disappeared into the night. Far away from what was coming. Peter and Eleanor would one day have her son and change the world.

Peter would know what to do about Alice. He always knew what to do, for he was the smartest and wisest person she knew. If her feet were on shifting sand, he was the rock that kept her life steady.

Standing in front of Alice's doorway, Eleanor saw that the door was slightly ajar. She looked one more time toward Peter's, then knocked on Alice's door and called out her name. She waited. Silence.

She opened the door farther and stuck her head inside. "Alice?"

Did that man come back? Is he still here?

She stepped inside. She held her breath. Alice lay on the floor, with her clothes disheveled. Bruises lined her face and arms. Alice winced as she touched her own stomach, stained with dried blood. Eleanor closed her eyes, vowing not to open them again.

This can't be real. This can't be happening.

Alice mumbled something. Eleanor could not keep her eyes shut. With blurry vision, she bent closer to her.

Through heavy elongated breaths, Alice said, "He roams through all lands... like... Pharaoh... like Herod... He thought he killed the baby within me... but he doesn't know about... the boy."

Eleanor's chest throbbed, and she studied Alice's face. "What are you saying? What happened to you?" She moved her ear closer to Alice's mouth. With moments of Alice's life left, Eleanor's thoughts slowed to remember events months ago.

Someone had told Eleanor that Alice had moved to Southampton the previous year after her husband and son were killed. She was poor and needed work. Eleanor had visited Alice several times to help her grieve, as she had no other family. She did not talk much. She seemed almost afraid of telling people secrets that, if known, could kill others.

Alice had never told her what had happened to her husband and son. Eleanor never asked her, for the pain was too new.

More blood spilled underneath Alice's hand, covering her stomach. The sand of life's hourglass was spilling out. How was she even alive after hours of bleeding?

"Your husband and son are not dead, are they?" Eleanor asked.

Eleanor had never forgotten what came next. Alice smiled and nodded, like Eleanor now knew the long-held secret. She gurgled, like she was swallowing something, and said, "We hid... our... boy. The one who was in Pharaoh is today within the one hunting after another boy..." Her eyes widened, like a lifelong secret unveiled before her eyes, and breathed out each word as if it was her last. "... *your boy...*"

My boy? I don't have a boy yet. How did she know I even wanted a boy? How did she know that God has promised me a son?

Eleanor paused to regain her breath.

Now I understand. Hiding. Secretive. Earning money for family elsewhere. She hid her boy! From Pharaoh?

Time was spilling out. Eleanor formed her words quickly. "You have a son. Is he safe?"

Eleanor was unsure whether to study her eyes or to turn her face away to hear Alice's final words better.

In her eyes. Fear. Hope. Joy. Dread. Then her eyes had widened, as if a ghost stood behind Eleanor. Alice grabbed Eleanor's arm, as if to warn her about something. A slithering noise moved behind Eleanor in the room. She had turned her head to scan behind her. Did a shadow move behind the chair? No one had stood in the available light. And then her friend's eyes had closed.

That was a night and day that still haunted Eleanor all these years later. Nineteen years later. On the anniversary day, Eleanor lay unable to move in bed. How could she prevent herself from remembering, reliving what happened the night after Alice had died?

Back in the present paralysis, she remained in bed. Resting. Recovering. Still as a corpse. Immobilized by invisible chains. Could she once again peek outside through the hole in the inner walls that imprisoned her? She could imagine messages of regrets written upon her walls by her own hand. They taunted her. She remembered the horrific thing she'd tried to do to her love years after that night nineteen years ago. How could she ever be forgiven if she could never forgive herself?

All these years later, she still wanted to move far away. But she was dead. She was alive. Trapped inside her body, breathing, but at times unable to move her corpse limbs.

Please do not remember what happened that following night.

CHAPTER 4

JAMES

England 1605

He loved to hunt above all things, and he excelled at it. The fastest and smartest of animals could not outrun the Master Hunter that lived inside him. Animal trophies on display testified to his power.

He hunted land for God's kingdom and prepared to expand His reign. Stewarding the most powerful kingdom in the world testified to his power. Future lands awaited his colonization. The eyes of James the Shepherd roamed world maps in search of an expanded kingdom for peace amongst factions and the safety and security of his sheep. Only the Shepherd, appointed by God, could protect the sheep from the religious wolves that roamed the lands.

Soon a town in a foreign land would be named after him to charter his name—a beacon on a high hill to light the path for the lost and wandering in the dark below.

But James was in no condition to go hunting later that morning.

The nightmare woke him, and he jumped out of bed in the moonlit predawn morning and ran to the mirror. His wife, Anne, already awake but lying in bed, did not even lift her head to watch him this time. The hairs on the back of his neck raised up as the Dark Light prowled in his bedroom.

James and Anne were not alone.

Staring in the mirror, he asked, "You can't feel what is spreading through my room?"

"No. You know I never have. You are in no condition to go hunting this morning. I am worried about you. How did you ever think that doing a cutting ritual with a priest in your youth would not eventually haunt you in your adulthood?" Anne asked.

James' words trembled in rhythm with his body. "I was a cradle king. I was king and powerless, dependent on regents and caretakers."

With fumbling fingers, he stopped trying to loosen his collar, seemingly tightening with a will of its own. "As a child, I often lay awake at night, afraid to fall asleep. Fearful that I would not wake up because my throat was cut. I imagined drowning in my blood. No one heard me screaming, as it was like I was swallowing water below the ocean surface. There were so many enemies. Look what happened to my parents. They were taken away from me before I can remember. How many people do you know who do not have even a single memory of their father or mother?"

He shook his head and covered his face with trembling hands. "The weight and burden of a distant God's royal blood flowed through me. I was a king at one year of age and later did not know how to rule against all my enemies, who hunted me."

He paused and turned his head away from the mirror. "I asked an absent God for help. When I was older, they taught me a secret of God. God withholds this secret from most people of the typical feeble mind. I discovered more to the God of the commoners than most will ever know."

Anne sat with wide-open eyes. James repeatedly fisted and unfisted his hands. "We performed secret rituals for God, and our efforts earned the reward of the secret revealed. I learned I am set apart from the rest. I am... I am God on earth for God. Extra power, not available to others, flowed into me from previous generations. I earned that royal power first given to my early ancestors and then passed down to me. He planted the royal seed of God's family into me to save those from the seed of the Enemy that ruined the garden in Eden."

Anne covered her mouth and remained silent.

He stood, as if trembling in freezing temperatures, and turned back toward the mirror. "The ignorant call the power 'dark' because it is hidden in the dark to them, but it is light to me. I call it Dark Light because it is invisible to the ignorant and visible to the enlightened one of God."

A sound escaped Anne's covered mouth. She removed her hand from her mouth and said, "Do you not remember that *you* obsessed about witches trying to kill both of us, and you made the witches pay with their lives after you interrogated them? You have given certain freedoms to the Catholics, Protestants, and the other groups. It all balances like plates on a single finger. You scare me more now than before with the witches. I am concerned that my worst fear is coming true. Is everything crashing down? I think you are wrong. There is dark, and there is light. But there is no Dark Light that is good."

He exhaled and stopped trembling when he recognized the man in the mirror. "The Dark Light is roaming. I alone am aware of it. It helps me. It guides me. Though it has no voice, it impressed upon me that it is roaming all lands worldwide, to find the one. The bad seed passed through the generations. The one who opposes the Dark Light. It ruined the perfect order of the beautiful garden in Genesis. The Dark Light works with me to protect my sheep from the seed's bloodthirsty religion."

James turned toward a slithering noise under his bed. "That is why I have great skills as a hunter. I hear things. I feel and sense things that others cannot. I will find him."

He narrowed his eyes with a broken smile. "You do not hear that noise? You can't feel it moving through the room?"

"I told you before, it is only in your head. Is this what you say follows you sometimes?" She turned her head all around her.

He smiled wider. "Of course, *you* cannot feel the Dark Light roaming."

He turned his head back to the mirror, trembling again in anticipation. The floor vibrated. The hunter in the mirror expected the monster from his childhood to materialize from the unseen to the seen. Or something worse.

The Dark Light protects me. Because of it, I am alive and have not suffered a violent death.

The Dark Light decided its own preferences. It sometimes moved invisibly and sometimes made sure James saw, heard, or smelled its effects. It hovered near him at times during the day and left no doubt of its existence within James' almost nightly nightmare. Or did the dream come from another source?

The nightmare that invaded and awoke him that early morning seemed so real. He initially thought he'd dreamed of looking at the mirror and was wide awake during the nightmare.

But he did awake in a pool of sweat. His ears always rang for several minutes after the nightmare, hearing the crying voices moving on the surface of the ocean. His hands always hurt afterward from gripping the floating ship debris to stay alive. The terror in his pounding heart confirmed the Dark Light searching in and around the ships' wreckage and floating bodies within his nightmare.

It searched—hunted—for someone or something.

Anne interrupted his memories of the nightmare. "Just right now. I could see it in your eyes. You were gone somewhere. Who is taking my husband away?"

The slithering sound moved from under the far

corner of the bed toward him. Sweat beaded on James' forehead in the cold morning. His heart pounded a familiar rhythm. He turned his head to his right side, expecting to see someone standing near him, as he could feel a presence gathering next to him.

And then a voice. "I have searched for hundreds of years, through every generation, for the seed that threatens my kingdom."

James jumped away from the mirror.

A voice! For the first time—it has a voice. He has a voice!

He clutched his chest. No one else was in his room.

Where did it come from?

James glanced back toward Anne. He did not even bother to ask if she heard the voice. He did not want to turn his head back to the mirror again. What would he find? He attempted again to loosen his collar. Would there be a monster hiding behind him with a knife at his throat in the reflection?

He exhaled with the familiar sight of the man in the mirror. What was happening this early morning? He'd rested in bed in the most lavish of clothing moments before. He possessed the finest of clothes from around the world, handmade for the one person they all loved. He sometimes slept in his converted nightwear made of the finest royal silk doublets and breeches. His royal clothing reminded him of his royal ancestral seed when he doubted in the middle of his nights.

He now stood feeling exposed, staring at his late thirties, with the effects of the nightmare still inside him. He often saw fear in the eyes of those who gladly loved him and served him under his reign. But staring back at him in the mirror, in his own eyes, a fear never seen before.

The Dark Light has protected me and saved my life before. I need him. I need peace. I need to find that seed. I need his power to protect me from a cruel death. Will he be there when the God of the commoners was not?

"Do you know who I am?" King James asked what slithered near him as he smiled with trembling lips.

Anne sat in bed with her hand over her mouth again, in the background of the mirror reflection. Before him, forefront in the reflection, a tall, broad-shouldered, strong man. The same broad shoulders that held up the most mighty of all kingdoms.

James dusted off the lower part of the mirror to see his hand. He squeezed and opened his hand over and over again.

My grip is strong... It is strong... If I just will it to be strong...

The veins on the back of his hand pulsated. A thumping heart pounded out a resounding war beat from his chest. It enclosed the gathering storm of a war cry, soon to emanate from him to foreign lands in a new way.

I will never die.

James trembled and pounded his chest.

The Dark Light communicates with me because I am the only one possessing the power to stop the seed that ruined the garden. This matter goes beyond just the crown and my sheep here. This is to save all of humanity. To save all my sheep.

James sensed that the seed of murder, the religious zealot, hid nearby. Someone was hiding the seed. James had to do something for the sheep worldwide, for their lives and security depended on him.

Was there any other alternative? Should James the Shepherd become weak and give up and wait for the Judas in the night?

No.

He must act before the Judas of the people acted. It was always better to be the hunter. The strong always weeded out the weak. The Saviour of the Bible committed one fatal error. He could have avoided his unjust murder if He had killed the Judas before Judas was born. Then the Saviour could have ruled the way He was supposed to rule. Preventing His own murder, He could have then killed all the enemies of His kingdom and freed the people from the Roman oppression and coming atrocities. Instead, He'd allowed himself to be killed? And for what reason? To allow the oppressive Roman regime to kill each believer one by one?

No.

All Judases must conform to further the kingdom to all parts of the world. There was but only one good seed from God, and that flowed in James' veins and in his offspring. God commissioned James to spread the kingdom. He would fail God if he wasted the holy seed of God planted within him.

There were new worlds to conquer to spread the rule of order and security that all people thirsted for. They wanted—no, needed—that liquid that gave security to satisfy the collective thirst in all. Safety and security were the only life-giving and life-preserving sustenance that could save the sheep.

"There is one that I seek."

The man in the mirror jumped away from the mirror again.

Oh no. No. The Dark Light is gaining strength.

Could he trust the Dark Light when there was no one else he could trust? Was there a way James could manipulate him to gain strength to protect his sheep?

If God the Father did not help His own Son when in need, who could count on Him to help His son on earth today? James had to seek more of the part of God hidden to the regular sheep. James would have to grab more of the Dark Light. But he could not take too much of it. James could wield the Dark Light as yet another pawn to serve him without it rising up against him like the religious wolves.

Anne had her head down, as if in prayer. The slithering moved closer to him. Something coursed through him. He stopped trembling as a power stirred through his body. It reminded him of a lifelong unmet craving for a food, then answered with unrestrained pleasure. He closed his eyes to savor it.

From his chest to his head, it then flowed into his arms and legs.

He opened his eyes to the truth in the mirror. His broad shoulders were broader, and his skinny legs were no longer skinny. His vision was crisper and sharper.

James smiled.

He does not know what I am capable of. He is but an instrument in my hands.

James opened and closed his now stronger right fist and drew blood.

The voice echoed again. "Find the seed... KILL HIM!"

King James reached out to Anne and collapsed onto the floor.

Chapter 5

CHINASA

Africa 1605

Chinasa and Abeni stopped talking. Chinasa's legs wobbled underneath her. Abeni's chest rose and fell with exaggerated breaths. Chinasa grabbed her friend's hand to steady her own unsteady legs. Chinasa's other hand was still strong and fisted.

They whispered to each other their strategy as the strange man stomped toward them, mumbling something under his breath. They would not run away.

The man groaned and labored, as if he was too tired to fight what was inside him. He raised his arms toward them, and when he was a grip's distance away, a short and skinny young man pushed himself between the man and the women.

The young man pointed to the women and said to the man with empty eyes, "You cannot stop this."

Chinasa pulled her friend away from the men but remained close enough to help the young man if needed. The strange one pushed his face against the young man's, nose to nose, and screamed as he alternated stares at the women and the young man.

Chinasa fisted her hands as Abeni pulled her behind her for protection. Abeni yelled and pointed toward the strange man and then pointed away from him. "Get out of here."

Chinasa observed from a short distance what was unraveling and escalating. *Is this all about me? How am I a threat?*

The younger man remained in the gap between the strange man and the women. He stood his ground, looking upward, eye to eye with the unhindered screaming madman. The women covered their noses as the man shouted with his mouth fully open. The smell of rotting flesh burned Chinasa's nostrils, and she gagged and bent over to throw up but was able to maintain control.

The young man's deep brown eyes watered but sustained his stare at the empty eyes inches before him. He did not flinch or blink. The man's screaming turned into a whimper. His eyes opened wider, as if he awoke for a moment, and a different light came and then disappeared behind his eyes. The momentary whimper turned into another growl as his eyes narrowed. He then closed his eyes with a look of defiance, as if to prevent the young man from seeing something inside him.

Several people gathered around the men, and the younger man moved his arms outward, preventing the crowd from attacking the strange creature. The young man pushed the strange man away. For the first time, the man lost focus with Chinasa and locked on the eyes that did not blink.

The one with the deep brown eyes pointed in the opposite direction of the women, and the man heeded. He growled again, turned to give the women one more stare, and mumbled, "We know who you are. We will find you—and your three hidden children."

"You're done for right now. Go." The young man spoke in a voice of authority bigger than his stature.

The man growled again and marched away.

The one with the deep brown eyes turned toward the women. "The two of us have battled many times before. I will continue to watch him. You are both safe for now. Go and help us prepare for what is coming." He turned and walked in the same direction as the strange man.

The crowd dispersed.

Chinasa shook her head as she turned to Abeni. "What just happened?"

Abeni shrugged. "What do we do? Do we thank him? Who is that young man? You can tell that he knows more about that crazy man and what just happened than we do."

"The strange man said we had three children. How many children do you have?"

"I have only my daughter," Abeni said.

"I apologize for my intruding questions. But we need to figure this out. Could you be pregnant right now?" Chinasa asked as she bent her head in reverence.

"No. I do not believe so. How many children do you have?"

Chinasa straightened. "Only my son—I do not think I am pregnant. Do we need to pay attention to a strange madman telling us there are three children he is after? I am wondering if we should hide our children."

"We need to focus on protecting our two children and figure out why God has brought us together. Let him think there are three children if he wants to. It is not like we can reason with him. And why should we? We do not owe him any information."

"I don't think I can handle things alone. We should listen to the young man who helped us. We are supposed to prepare for something," Chinasa said as she led Abeni to walk with her.

The young man seemed familiar to Chinasa. Such beautiful deep-brown eyes.

I know him from somewhere...

The women walked farther away toward the canyon. "Do you think the same evil in our nightmare is the same evil trying to stop us from talking?" Chinasa asked as she glanced behind them.

Abeni crossed her arms, as if protecting herself from a strong wind. "Our time together is even more important now."

After a short distance, they stopped. "People do not usually have a strange man trying to take them away. People do not have shared recurring dreams," Abeni said as she tilted her head and smiled a smile that soon disappeared.

"I agree. That is why I want to talk with

you—something is happening. It may have something to do with why people are leaving here," Chinasa said.

Her new friend nodded. "Before that man distracted me, I knew someone was going to talk to me today about my dream. I knew something was going to happen today."

The new friends held hands as Chinasa took three deep breaths. "We need to go someplace to pray. My refuge is the perfect place."

They headed to the nearby canyon.

"I know the best place for us to talk and pray," Chinasa said as she directed Abeni to the largest baobab tree in the area.

Her friend paused, whispered something under her breath, and looked up from the ground to the sky. "What a tree! I have not seen one like this."

She walked around the baobab, studying every part of it. She touched the tree and maintained contact with it as she circled it again. She kept her eyes on the top of the tree as she crouched down toward the ground. She moved her eyes to the lower half and ran her fingers through what was below the tree. "Do you know the story behind all the small pieces of wood under the tree?"

"My parents never let me out of their sight. Even on their deathbeds, they made sure different elders in the village continued to watch over me after their deaths. In my youth, I always wanted to come to this tree alone but could not. They never even let me go into the ocean by myself." Chinasa laughed. "As an adult, I have spent—many of us here in the village have spent—much time under this tree over the years. There is a reason we call these the 'tree of life.' I sometimes believe that this is a life-giving baobab tree."

Chinasa shook her head and smiled. "Whenever I feel lost, this place is almost like home for me. I am sorry. I got distracted. I did not answer your question. Years ago an older woman said that God was going to use this tree as a place for powerful prayers. She started to bring a small piece of wood each time she prayed. Soon we all did the same. All the wood came from the same special tree. That special tree is another story for another time. And now, years later, we can look back at a reminder of all our prayers. Some of them answered beyond our dreams. Some of them answered in ways that at the time were not what we thought we wanted."

Chinasa looked all around the tree. She sat down next to Abeni, on the small bench near the tree. "I can feel the prayers sometimes. Eventually, one way or another, they were all answered—"

She heard a scream from behind her. *What is that?*

She squinted and then opened her eyes fully. She turned her head. In the canyon, a boy ran from a man. Her heart raced. She stood up.

I know that cry. Is that Pada?

With her heart pounding, she had difficulty focusing. She prepared to run after her boy.

"Is everything okay?" Abeni asked as she tilted her head up to Chinasa.

Is that Okoro chasing him?

Through the blurriness, Chinasa recognized the way the man ran after the boy. He moved like Okoro.

She resumed breathing and sat back down. With a smile, she tried to relax her tired and sore muscles. Okoro and Pada played in the distance, not noticing the ladies sitting under their baobab tree.

"Yes... I think everything is all right. That is my husband and my son playing over there." She scanned the canyon near Pada to make sure it was clear. "I have never seen you here before. Are you moving here?" Chinasa asked, her eyes on her family and the surrounding area.

"We live many miles east of here. It took us a few days to get here. We are visiting a friend and her husband and daughter. I grew up with this friend years ago, and now we both have daughters. Every other year we alternate visiting each other. It is good for my daughter to have a friend."

Chinasa smiled after her boy fell and then stumbled back onto his feet, laughing. "How old is your daughter?"

"Amara is almost three years old. She is the delight of my life. Her smile lights up my dark nights."

"Amara. It means 'grace.' That is a great name. A great reminder."

"I was given that name in the throes of delivering her. Tell me about your boy."

"Pada—"

"—I have not heard that name before." Abeni motioned toward Pada, playing in the canyon.

"We named him Pada after I studied some Hebrew with some Portuguese friends. It means 'to deliver.' He will be five in a few months."

Chinasa laughed as she buried her head in her hands. "Hard to see him delivering anything. He only takes. He should be a king. He tries to rule over everyone and everything. Even us. Not too many friends yet for those reasons. We hope that someday he will grow to make the right decisions. But he has a good heart. Have you ever looked at a child and thought, 'That child is going to be somebody special'?"

Her new friend laughed and nodded. "I feel the same way about Amara. Other children are afraid of her, as she has had many injuries. At such a young age, she has already broken several bones, and they have grown back kind of crooked. She has had more injuries in her short life than I have had in my twenty-five years. Other kids cry and call her 'little demon' because of the way she walks."

Abeni paused. "We hope she is only slow in developing and that she can still learn how to walk like other kids her age. She will probably never walk like them, but perhaps close? She is already hurt, even at such an early age, by what the children say, so she sometimes refuses to walk. She's intimidated by what others think. She sometimes refuses to take another step if anyone is watching, even if it is only a short distance. We had to carry her the entire way here. She refused to walk because people might laugh at her."

They both looked up toward a bird screeching across the sky. "When I carry Amara, I feel like the best this world has to offer is in my arms," Abeni said as she wiped an eye.

"I have never told anyone what I am about to tell you." Chinasa gazed at the cracked dirt below her. "When I was a teenager, I had a vision. My mother stepped outside for a short time, and I stayed alone inside our hut, waiting for her. A vision of a man appeared inside our hut out of nowhere, and he told me some things."

"What happened?" Abeni tilted her head.

"He told me, 'There will be one who will come from you. He will be broken. He will be whole. Beautiful like jasper. He will rule with God.' And then he disappeared moments before my mother returned."

Abeni placed her hand on her chest. "That is quite a proclamation. Who is this that will come?"

"I never doubted that this would come true. Even before I met Okoro, I knew this would be done. I have spent my life waiting and preparing for Pada. Since his birth, I have protected him. I have always believed he would do something for God from here in Luanda."

"Could that have anything to do with the strange man? Did he have some way of knowing about this prophecy?"

Chinasa frowned, and she lowered her eyebrows. "I never thought of it as a prophecy. It would be impossible for that man to know. I never even told Okoro, because he would think I was crazy."

Abeni nodded several times. "It looks like there is much more to this story. I do not believe we have any idea how big this really is. Our futures, our families' futures, are at stake here. With the resistance we have already encountered, it cannot be coincidence that has brought us here together. I do wonder if the evil here, and the evil coming, is an attempt to stop the visions we have for our people and our families from coming true."

Chinasa rubbed her eyes and sighed. "This is bigger than us, our families, even bigger than the future of our people. I am going to tell you the dream that visits me almost every night, and tell me if my dream is your dream."

Abeni closed her eyes and covered her face with trembling hands. She wiped her fluttering eyelids as Chinasa continued.

"I see thirsty people drinking something that is not good for them. They are being distracted, drunk, from the liquid, from an evil that is coming. I saw two ships on the ocean. Some of the people on the ships were escaping. Some were taken away against their will. People and parts of the ships were floating on the water."

"Was there something roaming on the land, hunting people?"

"Yes."

"Were some of *our* people taken away from here into a ship?"

"Yes."

"Did you hear the voices of people crying out?"

"Yes."

"Were people... dying?"

"Yes."

"How can this be? Two people are given the same reoccurring dream? Why?"

Chinasa put her head in her hands and mumbled through her fingers. "Something is very wrong. We have been entrusted with valuable information to pray against and for what will come. We are to pray for the people on the ships."

Abeni lifted her head toward the sky. "Worldwide, we have all thirsted for the lies. We believed our leaders' lies when it profited us. They lied to us. They told us to hate the people they hated. We agreed with them when they pitted people and groups of people against each other. They played to our hatred. In every land, we have accepted that lie, and we then spread that same lie."

She raised her hands upward. "We are no different from people in other countries. We have all believed the kings who hate and resist God. We accepted slavery because it was somebody else's problem."

"It affected other people at first," Chinasa said. "We believed the 'It only affects them and not me' kind of thinking."

"Our leaders said it was okay for them to do what they did—they told us they only enslaved our enemies.

They told us our enemies were only haters and criminals who deserved their fate and punishment."

Abeni turned toward Chinasa's eyes. She covered her mouth with both hands, as if trying to prevent a scream. "They are taking some of our people away. Is the evil of our leaders now after... would our leaders ever allow... are they now after all the children? *Our* children?" She shook her head and mumbled over and over, "Oh no... oh no..."

They hugged each other and rocked together. Chinasa looked toward the canyon and tilted her head upward. "I will die before I allow anything to happen to my son. I know you feel the same about your daughter. I do not know what is coming. I do know that God wants us to be free, but He has a history of allowing his children freedom to choose good or evil and suffer the blessings and curses that come with that choice."

"Only He can turn what we meant for evil into good."

"It is rebellion against God when the powerful rule for profit and power. All I know is that our God rescues and saves."

"Lord God. Wake us up with a nightmare," Abeni said as she bowed her head.

Chinasa exhaled a heavy sigh. "We are to prepare for... something is coming. Something that we have not seen before."

"The dreams are an invitation for a role in the resistance. If we accept this role, we become targets of that same evil approaching. I am not concerned with my own safety. But my family..."

"I feel the same way. But the safety of our family, and others, is threatened whether we accept or reject the invitation. That strange man. Someone or something already knows we play a role in resisting what will be coming. I think he tried to stop us from understanding what is coming our way and how to fight it."

Abeni covered her eyes. "We could just ignore the shared nightmare, the sense that something is coming, our chance encounter, previous visions, that strange man, the young man who helped us, and just allow things to happen."

Abeni uncovered her eyes. "Or we could run into this with eyes wide open."

They both nodded.

"We are to play a role in some good coming from evil," Chinasa said. "A new birth. To move from death to life. We can run away with our eyes closed, but I say... I say we fight."

They prayed with the information given to them through their dreams and their prayer together. Near the end of their prayer, Abeni said, "We confess that we have allowed ourselves to be puppets indwelled with the hand of the puppet master that pits our hate within against each other. May we one day say, 'If God is our Father, then you are my brother.'"

Okoro and Pada stopped playing in the canyon and looked toward the women. Chinasa prayed,

"Where is my home? Where do I go? I have lived here for much of my life, but I often wake up with no sense of home. I feel homeless, and at the same time I ask, is this home? Is this where I am to make my mark? Where am I? Show us You. Save us. Redeem us. Show us a glimpse of home. Show us a new Israel. A new land! Make a new land like your Israel. Help us to see even a glimpse of it and one day enter into the new City. The City that is a cube mentioned in the book of Revelation."

Abeni nodded. "Break our hard land. Bring forth the new seed in new power. Even through a single suffering heart across the ocean. Prayers said under a tree. From a secret small house church. Even through those forced to hide or taken away into prisons. Move through the suffering in all the nations."

"Show us each of our roles," Chinasa finished.

They held hands. "I know you wonder where you are," Abeni said. "But I believe you and Okoro are like Joseph and Mary with Jesus, fleeing from Herod. You are to flee to protect a new seed. You and I need to work together. Someday, come to my village, for we still have work to do."

Breathe. Breathe. Breathe.

Chinasa looked toward the canyon and watched her husband and son playing again, with no worries. At a distance away from her boys, the strange man from the market stood staring at her.

It is coming. I can feel it. But this is home for Pada.

This is where Pada is going to grow up and change the New World. Our lives are here, but do we need to go away to buy time? Okoro will never agree to leave.

The strange man smiled at Chinasa.

CHAPTER 6

ELEANOR

England 1605

Sometimes people disappeared.

Alice's life as she knew it disappeared a long time ago. Eleanor had seen a man leave Alice's home the night before she died all those years ago.

Rumors reminded many people of the stories of the disappeared ones. Rumors persisted of the king filling prisons with those who opposed the king.

I want to disappear.

It was late afternoon, and the rain pounded outside. Still immobilized in bed, Eleanor rested while remembering what had happened years ago. Today she did not want to move. Another disappearing day dedicated to resting and recovering. Her ability to eat and relieve herself made it a good day.

Perhaps tomorrow would be an even better day.

Like the recurring nightmare of the people dying of thirst and the people on two ships, the memories from nineteen years ago invaded her head again, and she could not stop it. How did one concentrate on not thinking about something?

She decided to stop the fight against remembering that day nineteen years ago. The memories would invade her head with or without her permission.

Eleanor had discovered Alice on her floor, and Alice died shortly afterward. Eleanor ran to her boyfriend's home and told him what happened. Peter went to the authorities, and several arrived after a few hours. Their questions frustrated Eleanor, as they did not ask the right questions. They asked more about Alice and her secret past than about the mysterious man who'd left her home late the previous night. They did not even ask for a description of the man. Eleanor finally told them more about the man as the authorities were leaving.

But at least her faithful boyfriend, Peter, stood by to help her. She had planned on seeing him after checking on Alice and had put on her beautiful bright-yellow dress under a blanket for him that day. He loved that dress. She stood with her right hand covering the bloodstain on the side of his favorite dress.

He moved a stray hair back into place with the rest of her beautifully brushed brown locks. "I am so sorry about your friend. You do not have to be alone tonight. Stay with me tonight... of course in the most proper way. You can sleep in the bedroom, and I will sleep elsewhere. I want you to know you will be safe."

Peter wiped her eyes as Eleanor said, "I thank you, my love. I will be just fine." She held his hand. "I will need you later. You have much work today. Too much to be distracted with me today and tonight."

He leaned toward her and kissed her on her fore-head. "Please let me know if you need anything."

Peter smiled when she whispered, "When we get married and move far away…"

I need you to ask me to marry you. Then let us leave. We will find a place where we can live away from the approaching evil we have allowed. A place away from that nightmare with voices that descends upon me almost every night. Let us go to a new home. A new land. Apart from the ever-present king. All to prepare the way for our coming son so that he can one day do great things. Ask me to flee with you. Ask me to help you make way for our coming children and grandchildren and their children.

Peter kissed her hand with a glint in his eye and left for work.

One last investigator remained, writing some final notes. In the unknown gap of time between Peter going to work and when he would ask her to marry him, she had to find a way to continue living in secret from the Crown. She could never allow men of the king to know her secret plans of escape. Her future son's life depended on it.

But was it too late? Her people believed too many lies. A darkness that hid with what appeared to be a "Dark Light" roamed. With eyes, it seemed to be searching. That recurring nightmare showed one ship with people taken away and another ship with people trying to escape. If she remained invisible, they could not see her as a threat, and the Crown would ignore her. And she could escape.

Peter and she had to get married. She had to prepare for the first child who was to come—the little boy she had imagined since her childhood. During difficult days, this compelled her to continue to live. If she disappeared, if she did not marry Peter, her son would never be born.

Eleanor finished answering the last questions of the remaining investigator. She left the reminder of death and returned to the safety of home, but she could not ignore the ice-cold sensation trickling down her spine that caused the hairs on her back to stand up.

They did not want to know who killed Alice, because they already know who killed Alice.

They had no interest in arresting the killer.

He continued roaming the streets.

Later that night, she peered through her second-story window. Alice's door was closed. Night descended, and she prepared for the only escape available to her that night—into her bed. Having seen someone close their eyes for the last time made it easier to end her day.

A knock pounded on her front door, and she jumped. With her heart pounding, she ran to her bedroom window. From her angle above the door, the moonlight revealed someone's back.

Did the authorities have more questions that needed answers? Perhaps the last man writing those final notes really wanted to find the killer. Maybe they'd found the killer and needed her help in identifying the man who left Alice's home.

Maybe I can help with finding the murderer. I can help save someone else from being killed by that man.

Who stood on her steps this late in the evening? Should she hide and not answer? Did she forget to lock her door? She walked softly downstairs to check that her door was locked, but the creaking of her stairs announced her arrival.

It was too late now.

Her right hand shook as she reached to keep the door shut. She adjusted the blanket wrapped around her and put a stray hair back into place. She breathed in shallow and halting bursts as she opened the door.

There he stood on her doorstep.

The same man who had left Alice's house the night before.

Up close. Locked on his eyes. Empty. Familiar.

A man of the king.

"Good evening. My name is Alexander. I work for your king, and I am investigating complaints we have received. I was wondering if I could speak with you so that you could help me help our king?" he asked as he made jerk-like movements to adjust his clothing.

What do I say? Where is my Peter? If I shut my door and lock it, this man could in minutes have a dozen more men of the king come here and take me away for obstructing justice. I must act like I am no one to be suspicious of. He has to know I have nothing to hide. Just act normal, and he will have to leave. I can defend myself if I need to.

Eleanor cleared her throat. "Yes... please come in."

She allowed him in and closed the door. In the silence, they stood looking at each other. "Please have a seat over here." She pointed to a chair in a nearby corner.

He sat down and readjusted the neckband on his light-colored doublet. Eleanor stood as her heart pounded again. She placed her hand on her chest so he would not see her clothes jumping in rhythm with her heart through the thick blanket she had over her nightwear.

A back door waited behind the man in the chair. A large knife waited for emergencies behind a book on the shelf to her immediate right. He was tall and lean. Long arms.

He can reach the knife before I can grab it.

She remained standing.

The man cleared his throat and adjusted the front buttons of his doublet to align them.

"Oh yes. I am sorry," she said, almost losing her balance when she sat. "I am sorry. I am still recovering from what happened to Alice today."

The man sat up taller. He smiled with the left corner of his mouth. "That is understandable. I have some questions."

"Yes. Of course." She kept her hand over her chest.

He cleared his throat. "I started work for the queen years ago when I was very young. She taught me French, Italian, and Spanish. She loved God, and I loved my queen."

He paused at length to study her eyes, either to

make her uncomfortable or because he lacked the usual social graces. If a pair of eyes could knock on the front door of another pair of eyes, he was preparing to break the door down. She shut her eyes.

Can I get to Peter's?

He continued. "But a new generation came to power. People began to resist her reign, and she tried to stop those who threatened us. Enemies of the Crown, I tell you. In my opinion, she was not harsh enough. The commissions in 1591. Not harsh enough. Catholics were a problem. Dissidents are still a problem."

For the sake of Peter and my future son, I just need to lie to this man for the next few minutes so he will go away, and then I can run far away from the king.

Eleanor swallowed hard. "Why would anyone resist the queen or king when they are the source of our divine order?"

The left side of his mouth smiled again. "I saw the love her followers had for her fade with her beauty. She was losing her power. Very few saw what I saw. She sat in the dark, weeping and rocking back and forth at night. Her death two years ago devastated us."

He clenched his fists and raised his voice. "But now my dream for our beloved country has come true. A shining light in the darkness. We don't want what happened to the queen to now happen to the king, right?"

Eleanor's throat was dry and sore. Like someone had a grip around her throat. She could not speak and only shook her head.

"King James," the man continued, "now he is a leader acting for God. Yet we have reason to believe that there is a gathering resistance to the Crown. Alexander cannot allow this to go unreported or unpunished. Though King James has ruled for two years, no one has seen what I have already seen in him. Soon we will all see what I have already seen. I am not fit to be in the same room as this coming king. Alexander is preparing the way for the king's full entrance to fulfill the prophecies and to be our hope. I am a voice crying in the wilderness, so to speak."

While speaking, he adjusted his sleeve as it crept up his arm. Eleanor leaned farther away from the man.

He leaned toward her and moved his eyes closer to Eleanor's as she adjusted the dark-brown blanket around her. "I heard that they asked you many questions this morning. You told them you saw a man leaving Alice's home."

His eyes narrowed, and his voice became a whisper. "I have been appointed to find the leader of the resistance against the king. I suspect you will be of great help to the authorities..."

Eleanor sat in silence.

"You do not want to get in the way of me finding the leader of the rebellion against your king, do you? Of course, I could let you be of some use to me. You can help me fight against the resistance. Do you know anyone associated with the resistance?"

"Alexander... Mr.... No. Of course not. I would have

turned in anyone committing treason to the men of the king. Rebellion against God cannot be tolerated."

He laughed a broken laugh that made Eleanor pull her knitted bonnet over her ears because of a new chill in the air.

"Very good. You are right. Rebellion against the king is rebellion against God. My job is to... help any wandering sheep obey their Shepherd. To bring naughty children into obedience. I live my life defending the Crown, and I expect others to do the same."

His eyes narrowed and did not blink. "The king is seeking someone—not that we would harm him—but to help him and the others, to redirect them."

The man wiped his mouth and forced a smile. "Tell me about yourself. Are you married? Do you have many children to populate the fight against the faction that opposes the Crown? I know I am doing my part."

What do I say? Do I tell him about Alice's son hidden away somewhere? Or is it that the one he seeks is not even born yet? My son will one day bring down the king.

She looked at her feet and prepared for the path to the door. The man's eyes followed hers.

Silence.

He slurred his words while saying, "Only the king can give you what you seek. Peace. Security. Food. Shelter. Protection for the future."

He paused. He seemed to savor watching Eleanor shifting in her chair. The left side of his mouth smiled when he said, "I have access to revelations that you do not. There is room in our prisons. It has been revealed to me what you and Peter want to do. I know you both have hopes of resisting the king. I know about Peter's secret activities in preparation for your plan. There is no greater love than one who would give their life away for a friend... would you give your life for me not to take your Peter away?"

Eleanor leaned toward the hidden knife.

CHAPTER 7

KING JAMES

England 1605

King James stood, thankful for the power that filled him with strength and protection for his people. Thankfully, no one witnessed him waking up in Anne's shaking arms after he collapsed during the encounter with the Dark Light. She'd told him he had mumbled "The voice is telling me I must kill the seed" just before he fully awakened.

That episode several days ago embarrassed him but also strengthened him. A new sense of security filled him as the Dark Light stopped roaming after that morning. With James' new power, the Dark Light was gone and no longer needed. The mantle was passed. Like a wealthy father dying in peace after giving his entire estate to his only son.

Now King James could regain full control. He started first in his garden, like his God. He stood alone, basking in the glow of the morning light shining for him.

He possessed the finest baroque garden. It demonstrated life as it should be. Ordered. Symmetrical.

Designed. Enforced. All plants and trees trimmed and proper. Strong and grand oak and elm trees. Ripe orange and apple trees. Field roses created to pleasure his eyes, bowed to him with the breeze in their natural purity.

His garden was testimony and trophy of his power of order rightfully imposed on needy creation.

With the goats mixed with the rebellious sheep, James the Shepherd rested to gather strength to save more of his sheep later. Even Jesus went to a garden when His followers were too weak to help Him. The first Divine Right of all Kings fought for those who had wandered from the flock. Jesus fought for them in a garden—right up until His enemies came to take him away.

How did I miss that weed?

The king pulled out the weed that hid amongst his field roses. It tried to blend in with the life he planted. And where there was an adult committing treason, younger ones hid nearby. Could not a single young weed grow, infiltrate, spread its kind, and take over his entire garden if he was not watchful?

A seed of evil and rebellion existed. Could he have eliminated it before it was ever born? The key was to find the parents before the offspring was born.

With a strong right fist, he crushed and tore that weed apart. Drawn and quartered, King James denied the invader of his kingdom a proper burial. He left it to dry up and blow away with the wind like all the others before it.

He sat under the shade of his favorite tree. The long branches, with its low-hanging fruit, reminded him of many long arms bowing down before him, presenting gifts. He rested from the hectic daily needs of others under his tree of life.

A servant came and bowed before him. "My Majesty. My Lord and King. I sincerely apologize for disturbing you. The servant you requested is waiting to give his report."

"Ah, yes. I am a glutton for good news. Tell him to await my arrival."

The servant would have to wait. The king grabbed some apples and oranges and smiled as he consumed several before he left his garden.

The king entered his royal room with the servant kneeling with his head down. The king flared his nostrils. His heart pounded harder in his chest. He doubled over and bent down toward the floor, heaving, but nothing came out. He coughed and covered his nose as his nostrils burned.

No. Not again. *He has returned.*

King James turned his head, looking for signs of the Dark Light. No one else was around, as only the weak servant kneeled beneath him. Then something surfaced inside his head. Not his thoughts, but something placed into his head. Someone else's thoughts!

The seed. Do not worry about your sheep. The assassin is coming after you.

King James' knees buckled as he held on to a nearby table.

I can roam outside of you and through you. Even through your thoughts.

He clutched his chest and bent over, heaving again. He threw up what little remained inside him. He hobbled with what strength remained in his legs.

He is gaining strength. He is inside me now. He breached the walls I erected over my lifetime—a mirror. I just need to get to the nearest mirror, and I will be all right.

He hobbled to a nearby chair for support. He resumed breathing at the sight of his own reflection in the mirror. He moved his hand from his chest. He mustered a smile and squeezed his fists.

The weak servant remained obedient and still had his head down, waiting until the king addressed him.

The king straightened and aligned the royal coverings made for him. "Stand. Enough of the preliminaries. Give me a report."

The servant trembled, and his head bobbed up and down as he struggled to stand and keep his head up. "We have not yet found the murderer that fits your description. But we have rounded up many who have demonstrated rebel tendencies. We have found harmless papers with scriptural verses. They have no power when in the fire. Strange how they respond to their writings in the fire. Like lost letters from a lover. They did not resist us. I assure you, they will rot in prison before they threaten you. You are safe."

The king laughed. "Excellent news. I am sure the assassin, or the assassin's ancestors, lay rotting somewhere in our ever-expanding trap. With the seed within the murderer eliminated, the sheep can follow their Shepherd in safety. Be gone."

The servant moved as if escaping from a web before the powerful spider king awoke.

For the next several minutes, the king laughed as he ate his dripping fruit. Ripe fruit from his hands. His seeds. His soil. His garden. And now for his consumption.

What was I scared for?

James smirked. "So you can speak to me from within me. I can speak to you as well. What did I tell you? There is no threat. The kingdom is mine and soon to be worldwide. The seed that desired to kill me now lies unplanted, rotting away in prison. They are no match for the power that I have—which you have given me."

After several minutes, a different servant burst into the throne room. "Lord, I am sorry, but I needed to inform you. We uncovered new evidence. Those who commit treason are trying to kill you."

The king dropped his fruit. He loosened his royal collar. "What do you know?"

"Thirty-six barrels of gunpowder discovered under the House of Lords. They were waiting to kill you and all others. We think it was the Catholics. Maybe others? They would have destroyed you and Parliament! We have come to protect you, for there are other strategies set against you."

That nightmare. The nightmare that tormented

him almost nightly for months. People escaping. On the ocean. Ships. The voice wanted them destroyed before one rose up against his rule. But in the nightmare, he was in the water too.

Am I being told that the murderer is going to be on a ship? The murderer is still out there somewhere.

Maybe someone else could be the Shepherd. Even Jesus hadn't wanted to die.

This is the thanks I get for allowing the different religious fanatics freedoms? Can someone else take this cup?

But he was the one appointed to be the Divine Right of Kings. The King of all kings. Someone had to save. Someone needed to save the motherland. To spread the kingdom.

King James closed his eyes and ran toward the mirror. He mustered all strength before he arrived in front of it. That thing that moved inside him. It rose stronger this time from his chest and moved toward his head. He put his hands over his ears. He pushed his hands toward each other.

Push it out before it speaks again!

The servant stood paralyzed, watching his king. The king trembled without control as wave after wave of sobbing swept over him.

A foreign thought rose from his mind's ocean depths to become a voice inside his head.

King James screamed to drown out the Dark Light before it became a voice again.

But how long could that last?

Chapter 8

THE HEARTS SUMMONED
CHINASA

Africa 1605

"God is telling us to leave. He has warned me in different ways. Something is coming, and it is not good. We must leave," Chinasa said as she wiped her eyes, waiting for Okoro to comfort her. This was not going to be easy.

Okoro shook his head and stood without blinking. "We have always determined our own path. We have never allowed others to affect what we are doing. I don't care if others are moving away. People in the villages come and go. Luanda will always be here. And you want to move? When were you going to let me know you were this serious about moving? I thought you always said that this is where we are to make our mark. This is where justice would one day start for our people."

"I know... I know... but something changed. I can't tell you why yet," Chinasa said as she crossed her arms over her chest.

"You are hiding something from me," Okoro said as he raised his voice.

Chinasa and Okoro paused. The awareness of the sound of Pada playing and talking to himself between them broke the silence. Chinasa turned her head toward the east and half-closed her eyes.

Okoro moved to stand in front of her averted eyes. "Why do you try to control everything? You want to move. It is not your God. No. We need to stay here. This is where we are to raise our family. Pada has some friends here now. We cannot take that away from him." Okoro pointed to Pada, sitting on the ground in their hut and playing with a small wooden cross an older woman had given him at the baobab tree.

There was more going on here. Okoro knew something. "You sense something too—you have a deep fear of something coming for Pada, don't you?" Chinasa asked as she nodded.

Pada winced as a splinter pierced his hand. He cried out and raised his hand toward Mom.

Chinasa pulled out the splinter. "All I can say is that I have been hiding from what is coming here. I am sorry I did not tell you earlier, but I did not know how you would react. Sometimes I don't want to see your anger because then it makes me angry, and then we get nowhere. I can tell you that God is calling us out of here." She motioned eastward.

Pada wiped the blood off on the left side of his face and put his hands over his ears.

"The governing authorities have stabilized. They have promised help for the poor. No more of the rich stealing from the poor. The one out of a hundred now has to pay their fair share. The other ninety-nine has been doing that all of history. Punishment is coming for our enemies, and justice is finally winning. That is what you are sensing," Okoro said in a hushed tone.

She moved away, shaking her head and raising a finger for him to stop. "You have placed your trust in the wrong people. They hate God. Furthermore, it is even harder to get food. Some of our farmers have even left. It will only get worse."

With a smile and a partial laugh, Okoro raised his finger toward her. "Remember my promise. Eyes will open, and people will come back. We can now buy and take things that others have left. This is good for our family. Now we can get that farmland you always wanted. You know it is true. It is justice roaming the land, and it is coming our way. Finally things are working for us. That is what we have been asking for. You just need to have faith. Faith in what they are doing for our family," Okoro said as he gestured down toward Pada.

She aimed a finger eastward. "I put faith in God over government."

"I don't know if that is true. You don't even know if that is true. If you put faith in God over everything, then why the many rituals of trying not only to control us but God as well? Your squinting. Your three breaths. Your prayers by rote. Your God will not provide a job and food to feed a family if you have to manipulate Him to do so." Okoro shook his head.

She took three long breaths and pointed upward. "It is God that will give you a new job, and it is God who is the Creator of the food He gives to you. Why do you not believe that the Creator of all things is fully capable of communicating to us His desires? God is not mute. He tells us His desires that are for our benefit."

Okoro shrugged and lifted both hands toward her head and then upward. "Your head does not belong in the clouds. Come back to reality."

She shifted her feet. "I am the one grounded in reality."

He clenched his hands.

She squinted, then opened her eyes more fully and bit her lip. She could feel something in her mouth. It almost pushed down on her tongue. Words. Heavy words. Was there a way to stop the words forming on her tongue?

O God, shut my mouth if you want me to be silent.

It was too late.

"Like Joseph and Mary with Jesus, we have to flee from Herod."

Silence.

His eyes widened farther than she had ever seen before. Okoro laughed, but the laugh died a quick death. "Are you crazy? Please stop. I love you, and now I am really worried about you."

He walked to the other side of their hut and folded his hands over his chest. "My worst fear just came true right before my eyes. I always thought that maybe common sense would eventually set in. But now your beliefs in myths are affecting our family's future."

She walked over to his side of the hut, and Okoro moved to the opposite side. With his back turned to her, he said, "Where is Pada's mother?"

Chinasa wiped her eyes and hid her trembling hands behind her.

Where is Pada's father?

She paced back and forth, bent forward as if looking for a truth lying in broken pieces on the ground.

Am I going mad?

After several more minutes, it was too quiet.

Chinasa squinted, then opened her eyes wider.

Pada was gone.

***

ELEANOR

England 1605

Eleanor lay in bed in the dark of the mid night. Immobilized. She hadn't changed her clothes in days. She tried to live and not impose on others for help. A broken heart from a broken promise still beat in her chest. Not living with a husband and son away from the king broke her.

How could someone run away when they were broken? All these years later, she still could not forgive God for promising a son in a new home with a new life.

Her son was to one day be faithful to his wife, have children, and care for his family in a New World. He would one day end life in bondage to oppressive kings.

Life was difficult for Eleanor after that man of the king left her home nineteen years ago. Alexander grew in power, and her rage grew in power over the years, seething and observing him at ceremonies celebrating the king. When he worked hard to sit up straight and proper on his horse, she wondered if she should have grabbed that knife and ended his life—and hers in the process—all those years ago.

Things were never the same with Peter after that night. They'd talked a few times afterward, but something changed. Something was different, and they drifted apart over the next few months.

Several months after Eleanor and Peter drifted apart, there was that one morning. She'd lain in bed, counting her days left, when something compelled her to rise. Through her window, a beautiful young man and woman talked and laughed. They hugged and kissed, and the beautiful young woman helped the man with his belongings.

Peter. I have missed you. May God give you a great life.

Peter looked up toward her window, and Eleanor hid behind her wall. She clutched at her chest. She stood, unable to move as he left with his new bride. It was best not to know where he'd moved.

She never saw him again.

At least on that last morning, she'd been able to see Peter one last time. Her one love and planned life disappeared into the bright day.

Over the years, the ever-present ache in her chest made it more difficult to move. It was difficult with even short outings for necessities. Her activities outside the house occurred in the dark of dawn or the dark of night. Many days she ate less so as not to use up her food as quickly. For what purpose was life after that man of the Crown killed her and left her to rot alive?

She lay looking at the ceiling nineteen years after her life ended.

When do I have to get up?

Something slithered. The bed vibrated. She looked down at herself and gasped. Did the bed vibrate because of her trembling or for some other reason? Where did the safety of her days disappear? Things worsened into her lonely nights.

She could not control the shaking.

Something stirred outside her room.

Is it inside me and now surrounding me outside?

A new voice added to the chorus of voices that cried out almost every night in her nightmare—words coming from the other bedroom into her disappearing sanctuary.

"No... no... stop it..." The whimpering words pled with crying.

This voice sounded nearer. Closer than the

others. Her chest pounded and heaved, attempting to find air. She put her hand on her chest and moved her stiff bones to sit up.

"No... no..." the words echoed again.

Alice?

The pleading reminded her of Alice's voice. The first scream that awoke her that night long ago. But Alice was dead. Nineteen years ago.

Then something entered again into her head, as she had no defense.

Not the voices again.

The new voice and words came again from the other bedroom.

She pushed her hands off her thighs and stood up. She wrapped herself in her blanket and placed her hand on the nearby chair and walls to steady her walk. The slithering followed behind her.

The voices in her head stormed louder. The voice pleading from the other bedroom grew louder.

She entered the other bedroom.

***

KING JAMES

England 1605

The servant remained paralyzed watching his king. King James stopped screaming. He could not escape what was now in him. Where could a hunter run from the hunter within?

"The power within the assassin is growing."

Not that voice again!

James jumped from the mirror. He saw it right in front of him. The voice came from his own mouth. His lips moved and mouthed the words, but the words were not his words, and the voice was not his voice. He quickly turned his head side to side and behind him. There was no one beside the servant near him. James stood trembling, with his head turned away from the mirror. He tried to slow his thoughts to gain control—he did not want to turn his head back toward the mirror.

What will I see staring back at me?

He turned his head in a staccato rhythm with his eyes shut. Disoriented, he assumed he stood with his head facing the mirror. Should he ever open his eyes?

His eyelids fluttered.

There was no reflection in the mirror.

I am gone! The voice has taken over me. I am no longer here.

James was not visible in the mirror. The mirror reflected and warned of what would happen to him and his power if he did not heed the voice in his head.

The king desired conformity and peace with all the religious fanatics, and the voice demanded for him to kill the coming murderer.

He collapsed onto his knees.

God, help me.

He stood. His image returned in the mirror. His lips moved again. "The hand covering the murderer lifted. He stands before me, but I do not know where. It is too bright! He offends my eyes like a stone of jasper separated from my collective. It is a boy! A boy is coming to kill you..."

***

ELEANOR

England 1605

Eleanor followed the cry and entered into the other bedroom. In futility, she covered her ears from the voices now inside and outside her head.

She stilled, unable to move her legs. Then something sharp bit her stomach, like the fangs of an invisible serpent. She doubled over in pain.

Eleanor wrapped the blanket around her soiled clothing tighter and fought to stay standing.

Before her, Abraham. Her teenage son. Asleep. Lying on his back. Trembling in his bed. Turning his head from side to side. Covering his ears with his hands.

The slithering moved under his bed. With eyes still closed and still asleep, her son said, "No more voices... no more..."

For the first time, she saw her son, and not Alexander, in his face.

For the first time, she was not a discarded three-year mistress serving a man of the king.

While holding her stomach, her heart pushed against her chest in a way that it had not moved in years, like a prisoner banging on the inside of a prison wall, trying to get someone's attention.

Her chest warmed.

She was alive, with the reminder of a promise.

She ran and held her son, and she wept for her beautiful boy.

***

CHINASA

Africa 1605

Pada was gone.

Chinasa and Okoro had lost all sense of time amid their arguing. How long had he been gone? Did he run away?

Chinasa grabbed Okoro's hand as they stepped outside. From the hut's entrance, they looked in all directions. Chinasa tried to stand up tall. With her hand in her pocket, she gripped the small piece of wood she'd prepared for the next time at her tree.

She stopped in her tracks. A flash of a memory appeared in her mind. She was a little girl. A hand covered her mouth. She was heaving from sobbing.

Her arms reached out to her disappearing parents. Her parents screamed as she was taken away. Then the image disappeared.

Her voice cracked as she yelled, "Pada! Where are you?"

Her heart raced more when Okoro's breathing changed into a rhythm she had never seen in him before.

My fears jumped into him. Does he know something that I do not know?

For the first time, he mirrored her emotions. They ran and searched around the surrounding huts. Everything was a blur. The ground beneath her was hard and then seemed to shift. She held her chest with one hand and steadied herself on a small tree with the other.

"Pada!"

Silence.

Chinasa yelled at Okoro, who was moving in the opposite direction of where she was circling. She held her chest and pulled on her hair with the other hand.

"Go to where the boats and ships come and go. My God—I fear someone has taken him and is going to sail away. Go now!"

The strange man at the market and in the canyon.

"Run now!" she screamed. She took three deep breaths.

Okoro nodded and ran toward the ocean while yelling for Pada.

That strange man knows about the seed. He took my boy away.

She squinted, then tried to open her eyes more fully.

Okay—where am I again? Where is he?

She stood with her face in her hands, heaving for another breath. She tried to calm down, as passing out would not help her boy. Where would a little boy go? Where would the man take him?

An image of thorns appeared in her mind. Then hard ground.

The neighbor's garden.

New strength awakened in her body. It moved into her legs. Before she could run to the neighbor's garden, there he stood.

Like he appeared out of nowhere.

Just an arm's length away.

Where did he come from? Is he hiding Pada? What do I have for ransom?

Standing before her, the strange man with the empty eyes. And something else she could not describe within him. He closed his eyes and raised his arms outward, like he was preparing to receive something. From somewhere beyond him, a slithering noise from behind a tree moved toward the strange man. The slithering stopped underneath him, and the strange man trembled uncontrollably. An arm jerked forward.

Then he stopped trembling.

He opened his eyes and smiled. Then his smile

disappeared. "Your parents never told you. The thieves took us both away when we were young. They took us from our families. Your parents paid to get you back from the thieves, but I had no one to pay for me. They took me away and did bad things to me..."

He is a madman, but I know he is right.

Chinasa continued to scan for Pada.

Tears ran down his cheeks. His voice trembled. "He took over me. He told me to kill the seed."

Dried blood on his hands. Heart pounding in her chest.

No! My Pada.

Her voice cracked as she asked, "Who told you to kill the seed?"

"He is inside of me. He won't leave me alone. Just like in the Bible, I have to kill Abel, or he will kill me."

Chinasa surveyed the huts for Pada, or help.

The man mumbled in a different voice. "Is there an Abel? Are there baby boys that need to be killed again by Pharaoh?" He shook his head, as if to clear his thoughts. He moved his head down toward the ground and then raised his eyes to meet hers. "Is there a hidden baby Moses? A Mary fleeing with an unborn Jesus? Someone is preventing me from seeing fully."

My God. I remember the Bible stories. There was foretold a coming seed to save us. Cain was the first-born. Abel was born afterward. Cain killed Abel. Cain could not be that seed of God. Abel was dead and could not be that seed. Then God birthed Seth... May there always be a Seth.

His eyes rolled underneath his eyelids, as if he scanned inside of himself. "A mighty hand has blocked me from seeing the seed. I cannot find him—perhaps because the murderer of our future kings is still inside you..."

Stunned. Unable to run away. Chinasa stood up tall. She pulled out the Bible verse from underneath her clothing, written earlier at the baobab tree. She squeezed it like it was a serpent's head after it had bitten someone.

"You have something we want," he said as he lunged at her stomach with a knife.

She jumped back, and everything seemed to freeze.

Joseph... Mary... Jesus... Satan is still trying to stop a seed. He thinks the seed is inside of me. He thinks I am pregnant. Am I pregnant? He doesn't know about Pada. Where is my Pada?

Everything seemed to move in slow motion. The veins on the back of his hand pulsated. The arm of a strong man flexed. He moved with the force of a man possessed with centuries of hate and vengeance. Her stomach burned like a large animal had swiped her with a sharp claw.

He cursed and pumped his arms back and forth toward her, but was not touching her. It was like an invisible hand held back his lunging arms. After a short time, he bent over, trying to find another breath.

His eyes fully opened, as if Chinasa were a ghost. Or was there something behind her? He screamed and ran off, and collapsed after a short distance. He turned on his side to face her and reached out his arms toward her. "Don't let him take me away again…"

He stopped moving. It was the first time he'd looked like he was at rest.

Pada.

She lifted her bark cloth covering. She had a cut on her stomach. Bleeding. Was it a deep cut? No other injuries on her.

Pada.

The young man with the beautiful deep-brown eyes stood beside her. Then he disappeared.

I now remember…

It was the same young man who had appeared to her in that vision all those years ago. He'd told her about Pada one day coming.

How?

Pada.

She ran to the garden, holding her stomach.

Just a small amount of blood. God will heal me.

The voices crying out escalated in her head. She moved her hands to cover her ears.

The evil roaming all lands is the same evil in the kings seeking to stop what God is doing.

There—a short distance away.

My boy.

Partially hidden in the garden. Behind a baobab tree with thorns covering the ground and seeds in his hand.

There was no one else around. Then a voice. As if in the future. In a faraway land. A familiar voice... Pada, as a young man, cried out to her above the other voices.

"Mother, Father, please forgive me..."

She dropped the crumpled verse and lost control of her piece of wood.

Little Pada looked at the surrounding thorns on the ground and dropped his seeds. Most of the seeds landed in the thorns, covering the unyielding hard, cracked ground. And some dropped into a hole he had dug with his hands. He pushed dirt over the hole and put his hands to his ears. With tears dripping from his eyes onto the covered seeds, he turned to Chinasa and uncovered his ears.

"We should pray for a man in prison."

He covered his ears again and shook his head back and forth. "They are crying out to me again."

Something slithered behind a bush nearby.

Chinasa ran and stood in the gap between the slithering noise and Pada. She winced with the cuts on her feet. She turned her back to the bush, as if shielding him from a cold, strong ocean wind trying to take him away. She pulled Pada up into her arms.

The voices quieted.

Pada wiped her eyes with a hand.

Chinasa smiled and said, "I love you. You are right. We need to pray for the man in prison, for he will help to free many people."

She held him with all the love given to her to give

away. At that moment, no thief could rip him out of her arms.

An ocean bird flew above them and headed toward the sea.

In the canyon, a young man with beautiful deep-brown eyes stepped barefoot on the resisting thorns. He placed three small pieces of wood at the base of the baobab tree and a fourth one behind them.

ABOUT THE AUTHOR

As a storyteller and a physical therapist, Charles Anthony Solorio works with people who are physically and sometimes emotionally broken. He believes that stories can confront the raw side of our brokenness and bring about healing by seeing our own lives through the lenses of both faith and a faithfulness woven into our history. *New Seed and Hard Ground* is Charles' debut fictional book. Charles lives in Southern California with his wife and adult children. You can meet Charlie at **charlesanthonysolorio.com**